THE BIG RESPONSIBILITY
Part of the "John and Scott Leadership Series for Children"
SCOTT BRINKLEY

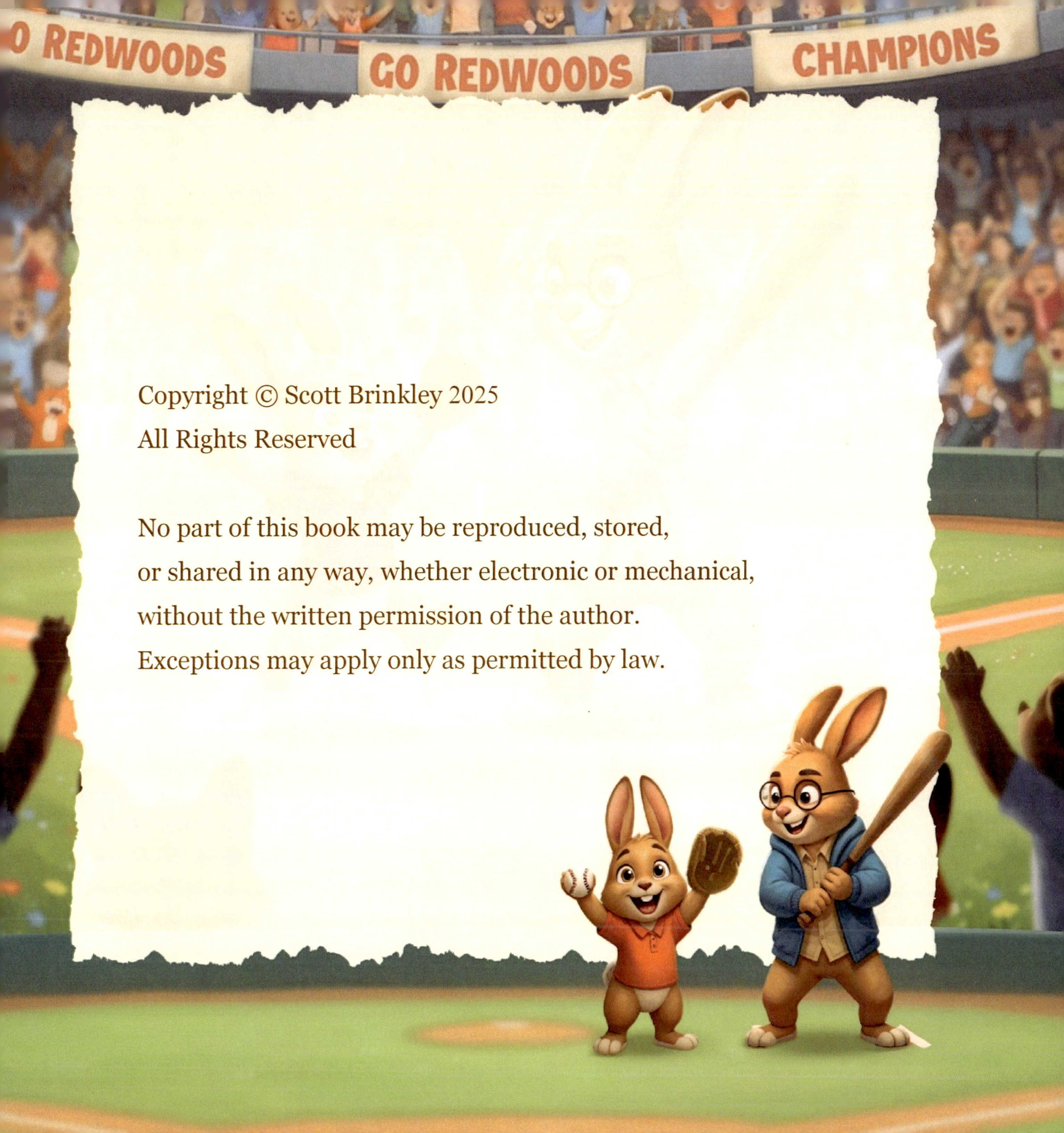

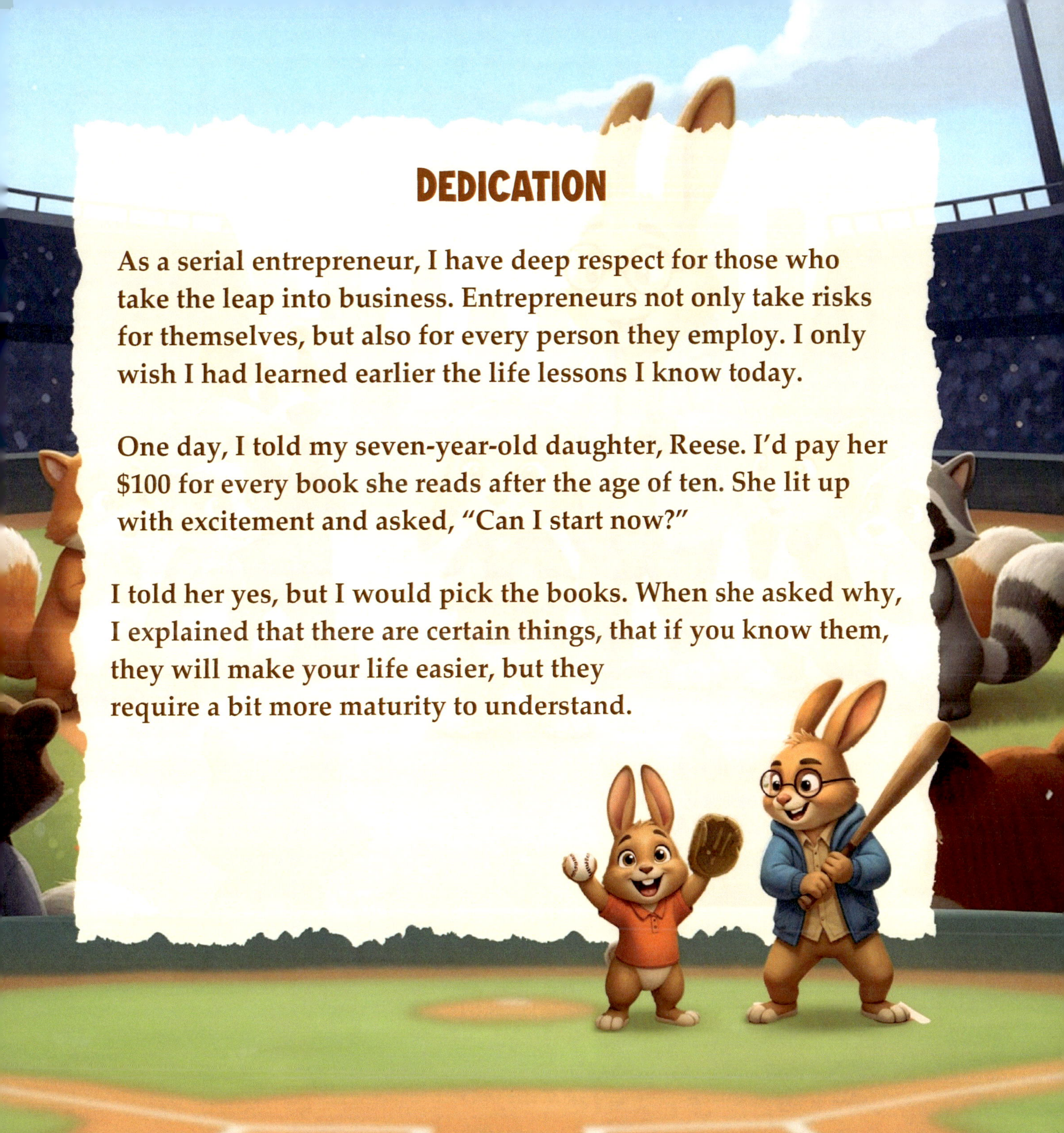

DEDICATION

As a serial entrepreneur, I have deep respect for those who take the leap into business. Entrepreneurs not only take risks for themselves, but also for every person they employ. I only wish I had learned earlier the life lessons I know today.

One day, I told my seven-year-old daughter, Reese. I'd pay her $100 for every book she reads after the age of ten. She lit up with excitement and asked, "Can I start now?"

I told her yes, but I would pick the books. When she asked why, I explained that there are certain things, that if you know them, they will make your life easier, but they require a bit more maturity to understand.

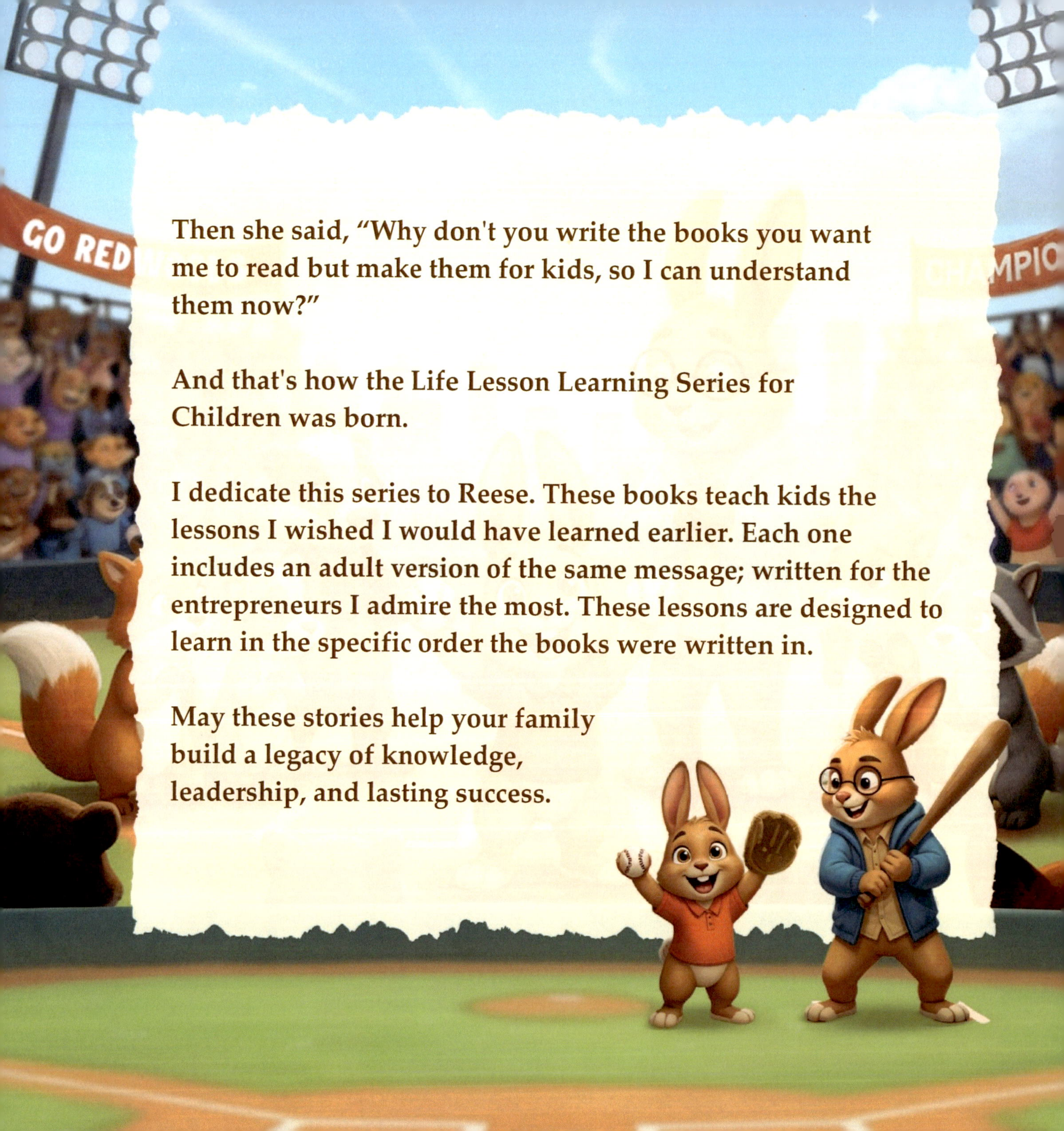

Then she said, "Why don't you write the books you want me to read but make them for kids, so I can understand them now?"

And that's how the Life Lesson Learning Series for Children was born.

I dedicate this series to Reese. These books teach kids the lessons I wished I would have learned earlier. Each one includes an adult version of the same message; written for the entrepreneurs I admire the most. These lessons are designed to learn in the specific order the books were written in.

May these stories help your family build a legacy of knowledge, leadership, and lasting success.

In a sunny meadow, two rabbits named Scott and John were the best of friends.

They did everything together, building forts, racing through fields and even running their own Bunny Baseball team.

One morning, the whole meadow gathered for the big
Bunny Baseball Championship game.

Scott and John's team, The Redwoods, was ready.

John was the captain, and Scott was the pitcher.

GO REDWOODS
GO REDWOODS
2025 CHAMPION

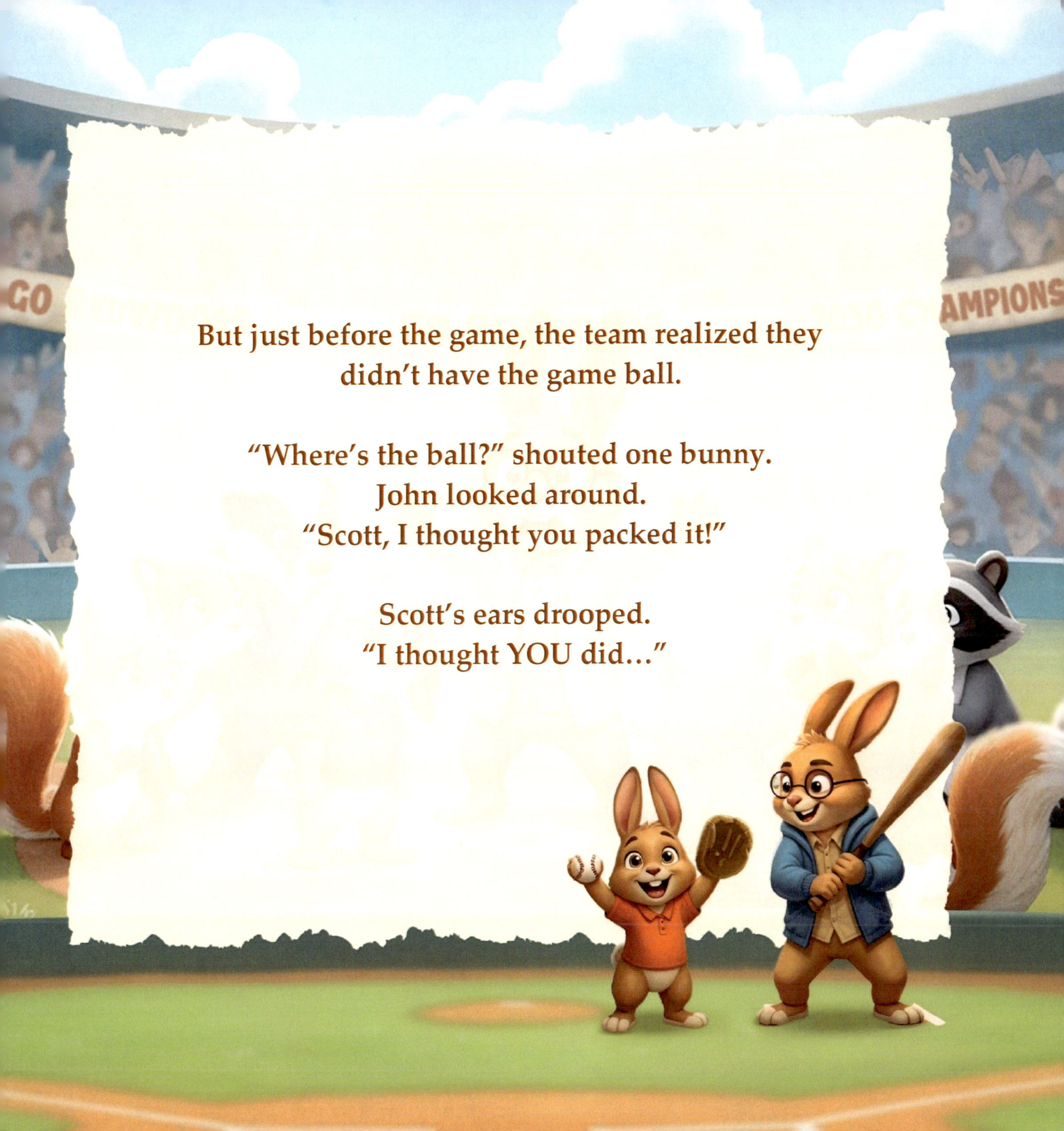
But just before the game, the team realized they
didn't have the game ball.

"Where's the ball?" shouted one bunny.
John looked around.
"Scott, I thought you packed it!"

Scott's ears drooped.
"I thought YOU did…"

GO REDWOODS
GO REDWOODS
2030 CHAMPIO

The game was rescheduled for the next day.
The crowd went home disappointed.

The team was upset. Scott frowned and said,
"It's not my fault!

Someone else should have
reminded me!"

GO REDWOODS
GO REDWOODS
GO REDWOODS

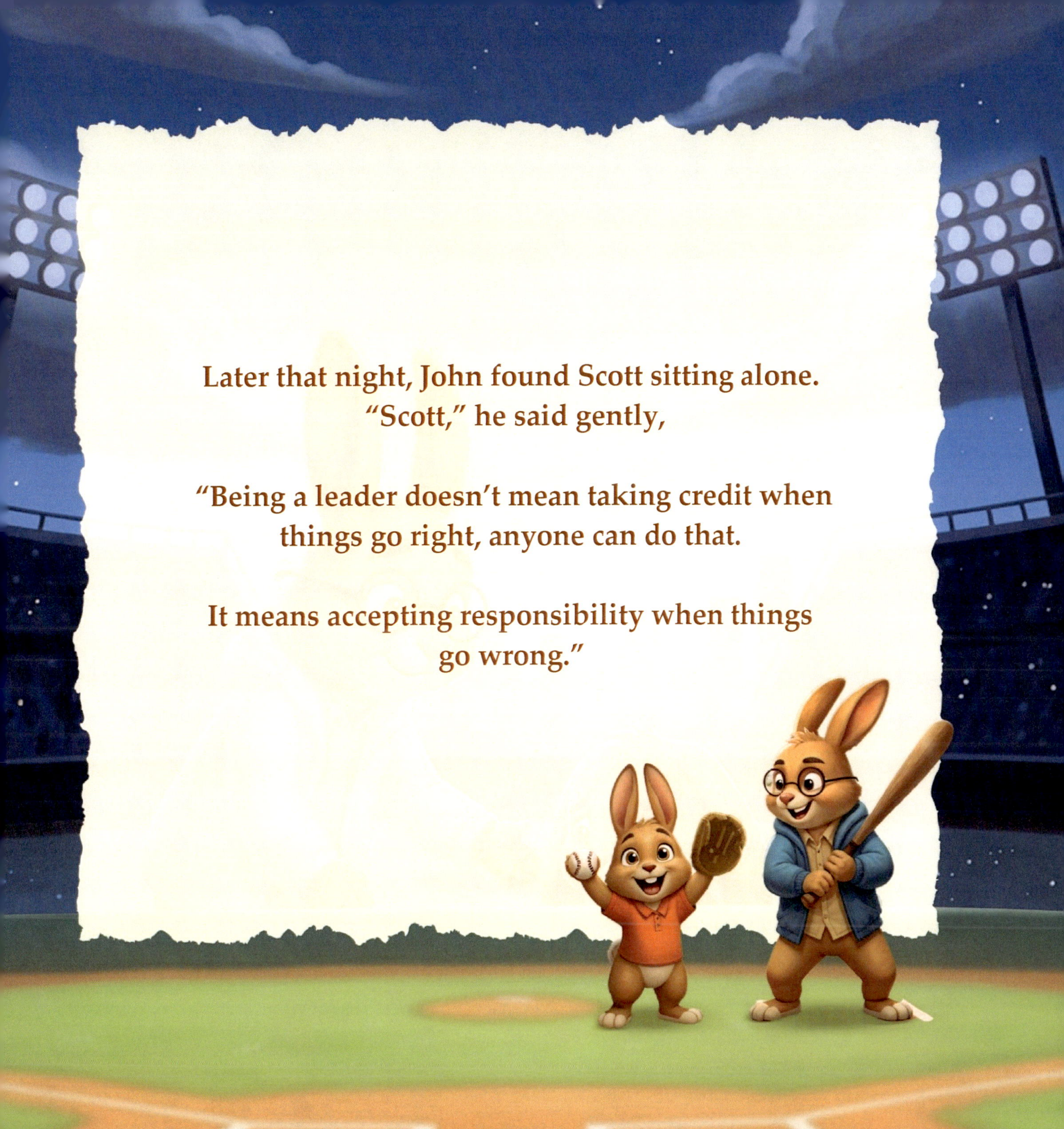

Later that night, John found Scott sitting alone.
"Scott," he said gently,

"Being a leader doesn't mean taking credit when
things go right, anyone can do that.

It means accepting responsibility when things
go wrong."

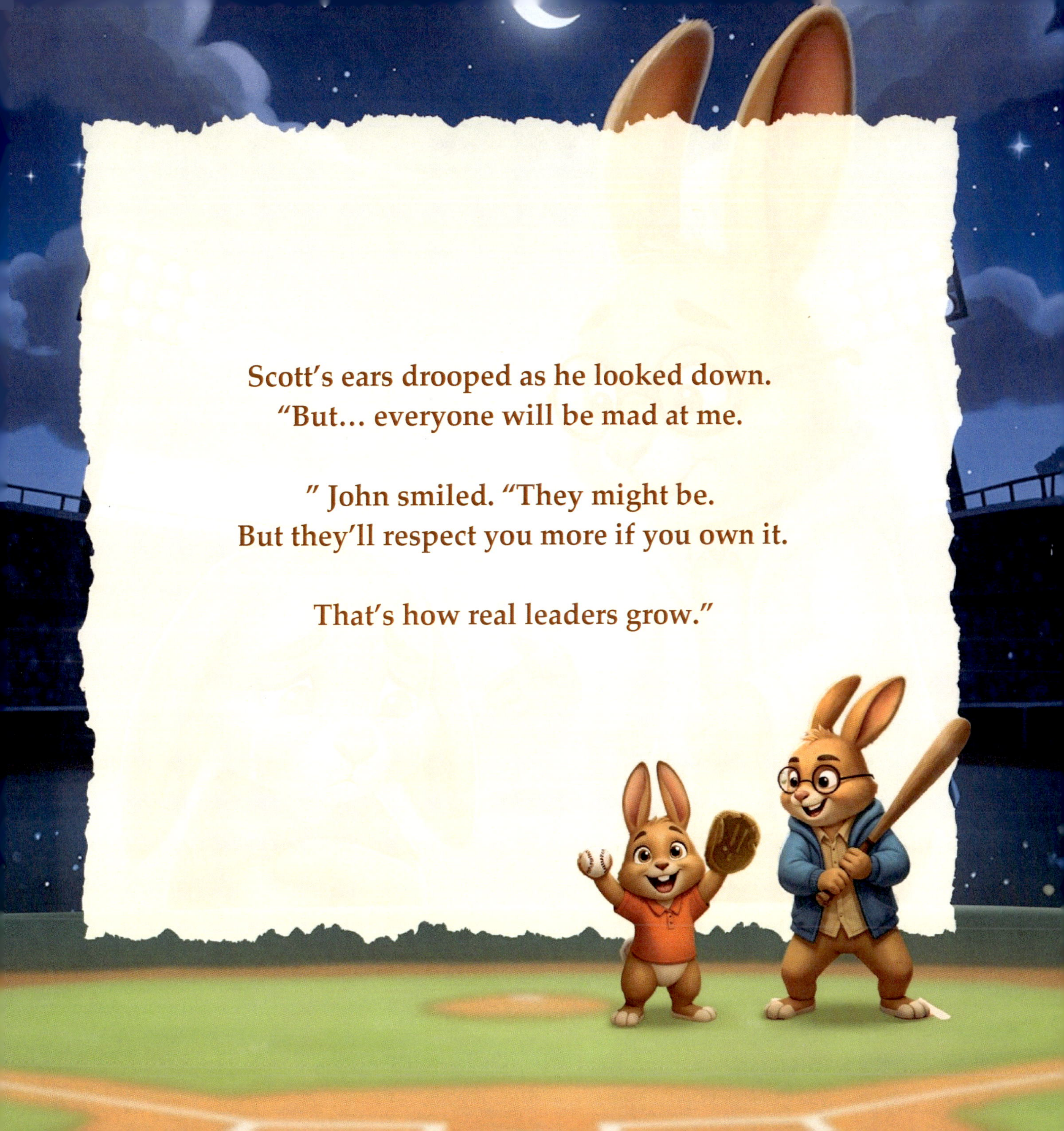

Scott's ears drooped as he looked down.
"But… everyone will be mad at me.

" John smiled. "They might be.
But they'll respect you more if you own it.

That's how real leaders grow."

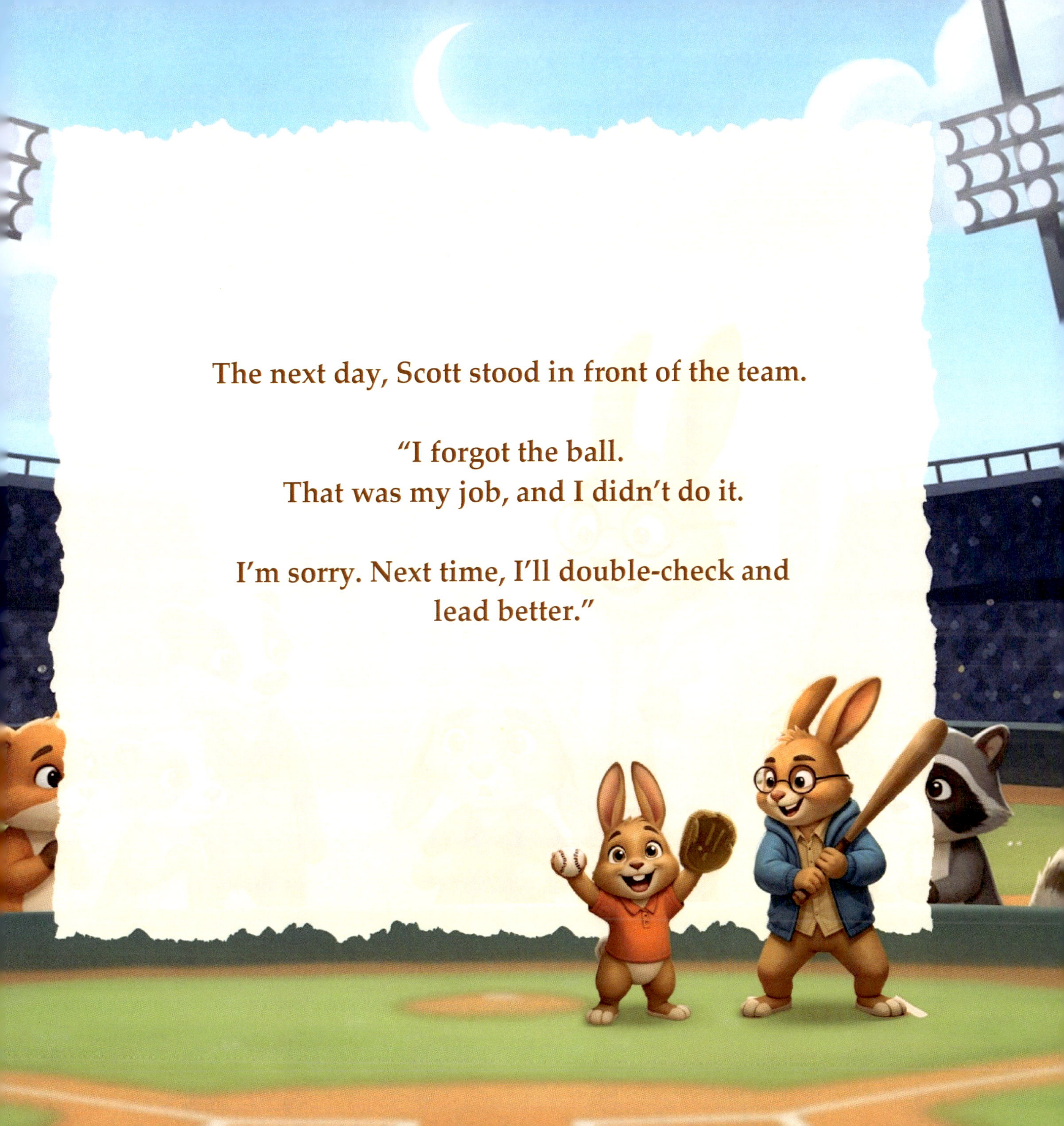

The next day, Scott stood in front of the team.

"I forgot the ball.
That was my job, and I didn't do it.

I'm sorry. Next time, I'll double-check and
lead better."

The team looked surprised,
but then they all smiled.

"Thanks, Scott," one bunny said.
"That's what a real leader sounds like."

The team forgave him.
Then Scott pulled out two baseballs,
just in case.

And when they played,
they played their hearts out.

GO REDWOODS
2025 CHAMPIO

From that day on, Scott wasn't just a player.
He was on his way to becoming a great leader.

Because he learned that great leaders take full
responsibility and accountability for their actions
when things go wrong.

GO REDWOODS
2025 CHA

THE LESSON

When I was 15 years old, my father was teaching me how to drive. I'll never forget sitting at a stop sign, about to pull out onto Walton Ferry Road. As I eased forward, a car came from my left and slammed on its brakes, tires screeching.

My heart pounded, sweat beaded on my forehead, and anxiety took over. The man in the other car threw his hands in the air, yelling at the top of his lungs.

No one was hurt, and he drove away but my nerves were shot. I pulled into a gas station to calm down.

In my mind, I'd just come inches from killing both myself and my dad.

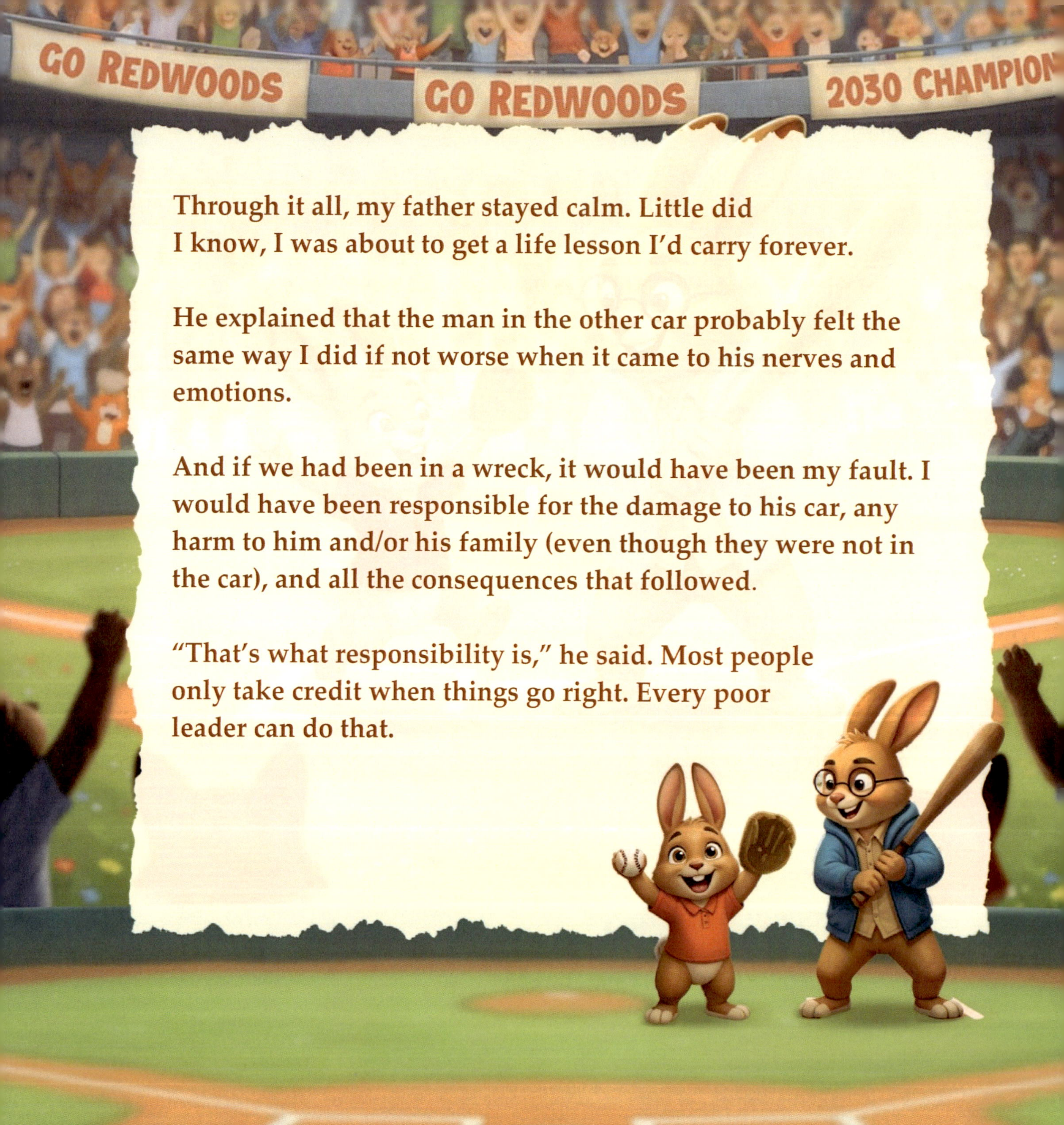

Through it all, my father stayed calm. Little did I know, I was about to get a life lesson I'd carry forever.

He explained that the man in the other car probably felt the same way I did if not worse when it came to his nerves and emotions.

And if we had been in a wreck, it would have been my fault. I would have been responsible for the damage to his car, any harm to him and/or his family (even though they were not in the car), and all the consequences that followed.

"That's what responsibility is," he said. Most people only take credit when things go right. Every poor leader can do that.

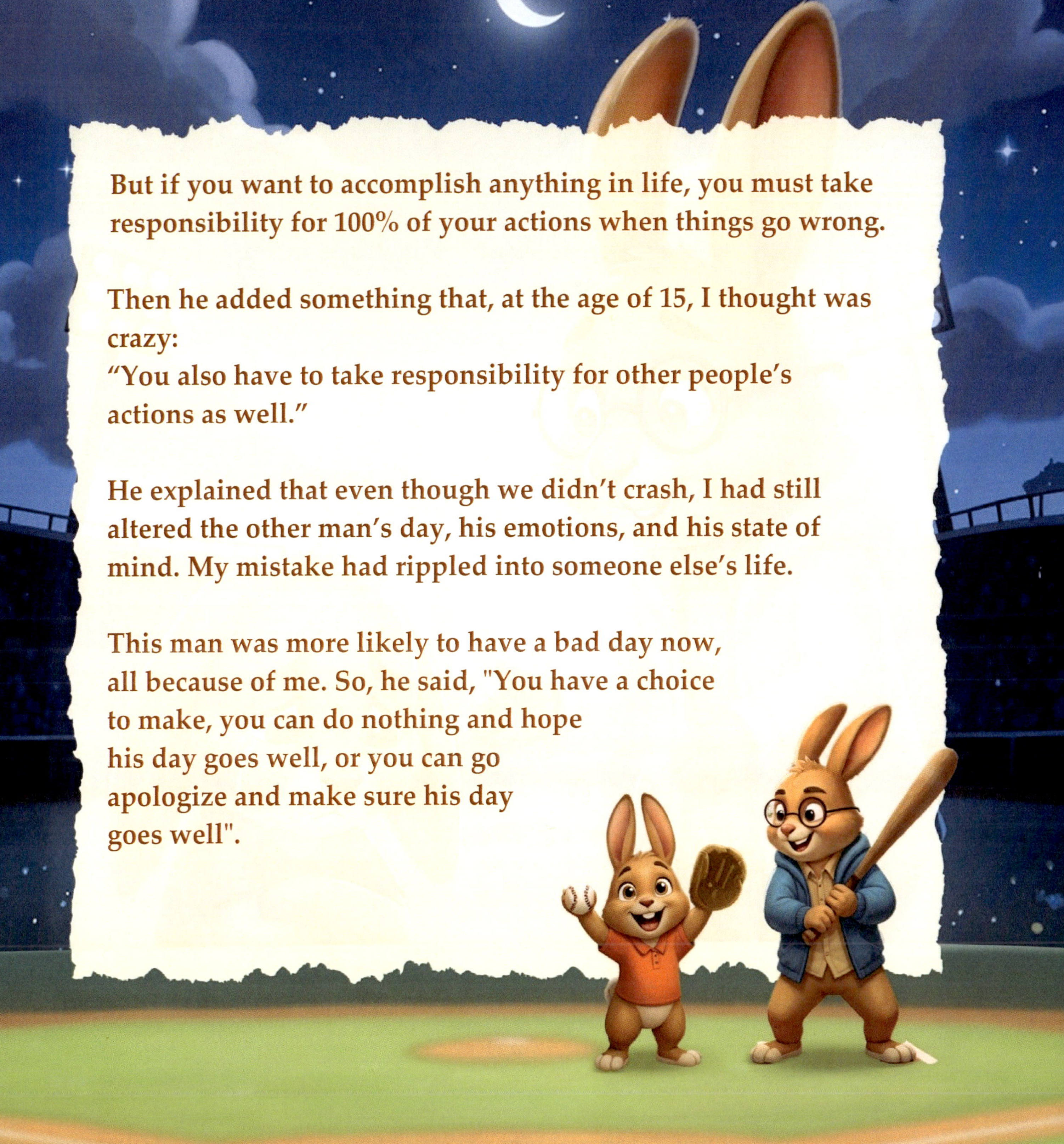

But if you want to accomplish anything in life, you must take responsibility for 100% of your actions when things go wrong.

Then he added something that, at the age of 15, I thought was crazy:
"You also have to take responsibility for other people's actions as well."

He explained that even though we didn't crash, I had still altered the other man's day, his emotions, and his state of mind. My mistake had rippled into someone else's life.

This man was more likely to have a bad day now, all because of me. So, he said, "You have a choice to make, you can do nothing and hope his day goes well, or you can go apologize and make sure his day goes well".

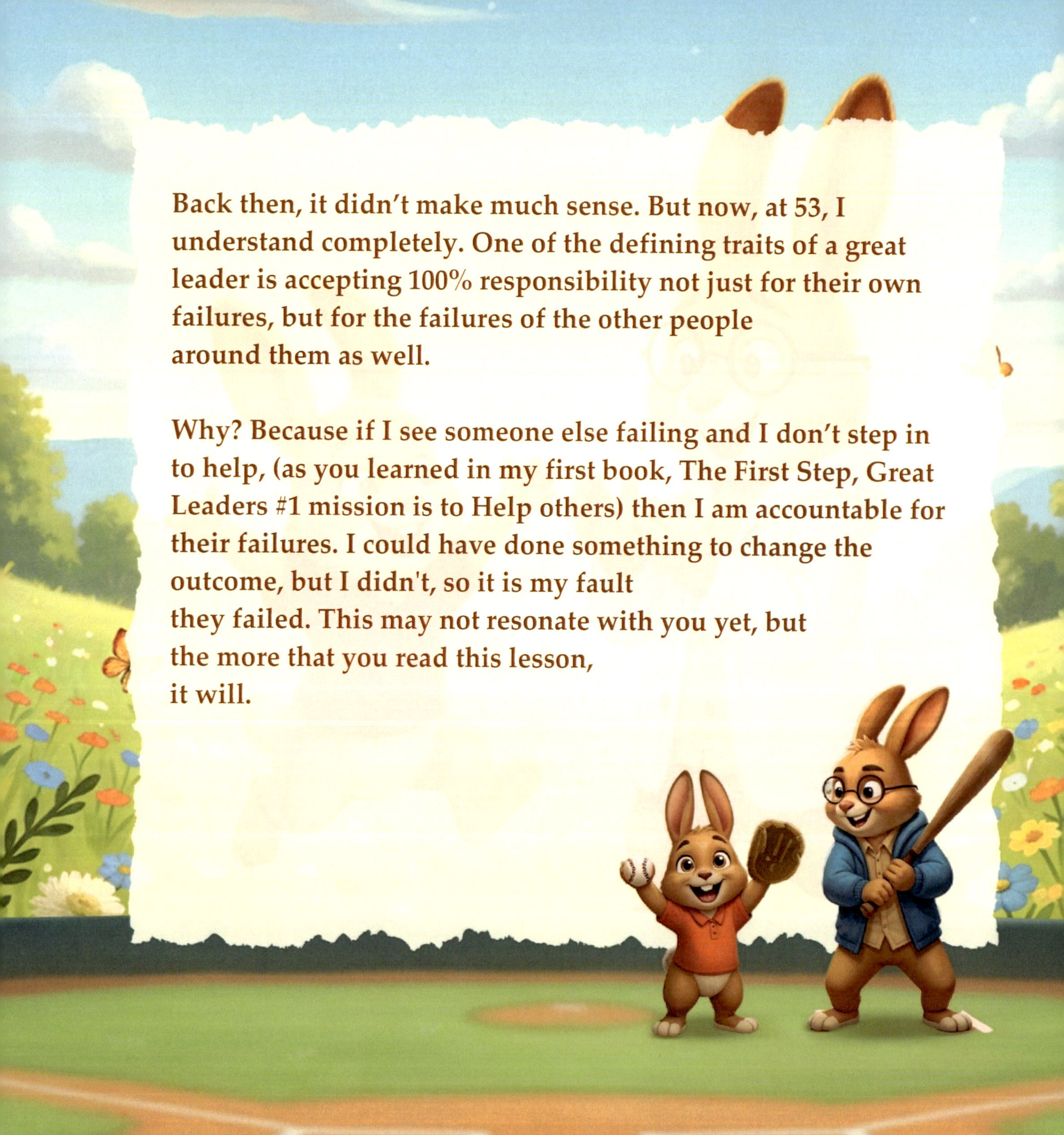
Back then, it didn't make much sense. But now, at 53, I understand completely. One of the defining traits of a great leader is accepting 100% responsibility not just for their own failures, but for the failures of the other people around them as well.

Why? Because if I see someone else failing and I don't step in to help, (as you learned in my first book, The First Step, Great Leaders #1 mission is to Help others) then I am accountable for their failures. I could have done something to change the outcome, but I didn't, so it is my fault they failed. This may not resonate with you yet, but the more that you read this lesson, it will.

My hope is that this book helps you grow as an entrepreneur and pass this lesson on to your kids.

If they make accepting 100% responsibility and accountability of not only their failures but everyone else's around them as well,

I will say with full confidence:
They'll live a richer, more fulfilling life.

GO REDWOODS
GO REDWOODS
2030 CHAMPION
THE END

I want to take a moment to personally thank you for not only purchasing this book, but for investing in yourself and in your children, the next generation of leaders.

By reading The Big Responsibility, you're not only learning and growing you're also planting seeds that will shape the future through your children.

That's something powerful, and I don't take it lightly.

Writing this book has been a joy for me, but what makes it meaningful is knowing it's being used by families like yours.

My hope is that the lessons inside have been helpful, inspiring, and practical.

If you enjoyed the book, it would mean the world to me if you'd take a moment to scan the QR code, leave me a 5 Star review and share your thoughts online.

Your feedback not only helps me, but it also helps other families discover this resource for their own journey.

With appreciation,

Scott Brinkley.